KIDZ
RADIO™

More
FIVE-MINUTE
MYSTERIES
Sleuth Book™

KEN WEBER

RUNNING PRESS
PHILADELPHIA • LONDON

9   8   7   6   5   4   3   2   1

Digit on the right indicates the number of this printing.

ISBN 1–56138–723–1 (package)

Cover illustration by Wally Neibart
Interior illustrations by Len Epstein
Cover and interior design by Corinda J. Cook
Edited by Tara Ann McFadden

Printed in the United States

This book may be ordered by mail from the publisher.
Please add $2.50 for postage and handling.
But try your bookstore first!

Running Press Book Publishers
125 South Twenty-second Street
Philadelphia, Pennsylvania 19103–4399

Contents

Introduction

Hi kids! Welcome to another KIDZ RADIO™ show. This is Ken Weber with MORE FIVE-MINUTE MYSTERIES. If you have the first book in this series, then you know how this works. In these stories, you get to be a detective, a sleuth, a solver of mysteries. What you do first, is listen to a story on the tape. At the end of the story, we give you a question, a mystery to solve. After you hear the question you can press the pause button and think for a minute. Or, if you want, rewind the tape and listen to the story again to make sure you have all the clues. A lot of our detectives do that.

When you think you have solved the mystery, start the tape again and our answer will follow right away. If you get stuck, there are some hints at the back of the book. But don't look at them until you really have to.

Got the idea? Okay, here's the first mystery, "The Case of the Blue Tattoo." It's about arresting the right person in a shoplifting case. Listen carefully. Remember to rewind and listen again if you want to. By the way, every mystery on the tape is also in the book. Some detectives find that its fun to read along. We think it helps too.

Here goes now! Good luck, and have fun!

① The Case of the Blue Tattoo

NARRATOR: Officer Tammy Ticket walks across the busy police station toward an interview room. Inside that room, a witness is waiting for her. His name is Lester Gray. It was Lester Gray who saw a shoplifter steal a hairdryer at McFadden's Drug Store.

TAMMY TICKET: Good afternoon, Mr. Gray. Thank you for coming in. I'm Officer Ticket.

LESTER GRAY: How do you do, Officer? I saw the man who stole a hairdryer and I'm here to point him out to you. When do we start?

TAMMY TICKET: Right now, Mr. Gray. Now, behind you—don't turn around yet!—There's a one-way mirror in the wall.

LESTER GRAY: Yes. . . .

TAMMY TICKET: When you turn around, I want you to look through that window at the five people lined up in the next room. Each of them has a blue tattoo on one arm. You know what happens in a police lineup, don't you?

LESTER GRAY: Of course I do. I have to look at the people in there and tell you which is the one I saw taking the hairdryer. Um . . . they can't see me, can they?

TAMMY TICKET: No. It's one-way glass. Now, before you turn around, let's be sure I have all the facts. You didn't see the shoplifter's face, did you? You just saw him from the neck down, isn't that right?

LESTER GRAY: Yes, that's right. But there'll be no trouble picking him out because of the tattoo. You see, I was standing in Aisle Four. The hairdryers are in Aisle Three. But with those big round mirrors, you know, at the end of the aisle? Up on the wall? You can see everything. Anyway. I'm standing in

Aisle Four, I look up at the mirror. And I see this man. Kind of chubby. I notice him because on the right he's got this really big blue tattoo. And what happens? He reaches out with that tattooed arm, grabs a hairdryer off the shelf and it disappears into the front of his shirt. The hairdryer, not the shelf!

TAMMY TICKET: Very well, Mr. Gray. Then I guess it's time to turn around. Do you see your shoplifter in there?

LESTER GRAY: Mmmm. They're all men. That's right. All kind of chubby . . . shoplifter was chubby. They all have blue tattoos on one arm. Really, Officer, this is very easy. There's only one man in there with a tattoo on his right arm. He's got to be the shoplifter!

TAMMY TICKET: Not quite, Mr. Gray, not quite. I was afraid of this. Guess it isn't going to be an easy case after all.

Why does Officer Tammy Ticket believe that Mr. Gray has picked the wrong person out of the lineup?

If you need a hint, please turn to page 54. For the solution, turn to page 58.

2 The Case of Mr. Comatosa's Nightmare

MRS. COMATOSA: Sergeant, for goodness sake. Twelve hours ago my husband died of a heart attack. Can't I just go home and deal with that? I want to be with my family. I've already told two other officers everything I know. Surely I don't have to do it again.

SERGEANT: Just once more, please, Mrs. Comatosa. I have to tape it. I'm sorry for your loss, but. . . . Now, as I understand it, you and your husband had gone to bed as usual?

MRS. COMATOSA: Oh, all right. Yes, we went to bed as usual at eleven o'clock. It was about one in the morning when he had this terrible nightmare.

In the nightmare we were out in a boat, you see, way out in the ocean. Tuna fishing. He likes . . . er . . . used to like tuna fishing. We've been at least a dozen times since he won the lottery. In the dream, a big shark came up to the boat. Huge. As big as the boat! And it rammed us!

The captain tried to start the engine and get out of there but it wouldn't start. And the shark kept ramming and

ramming and the boat started to sink. You can imagine how frightening, and with my husband's bad heart and all, that's what must have brought on the heart attack. You see, I recognized that he was having a heart attack because he had one last year just like it. Except that this one . . . well, you know what happened this time. Now can I go?

SERGEANT: I'm afraid not, Mrs. Comatosa. The shark isn't the only fishy part of your story.

What is "fishy" about Mrs. Comatosa's story?
Why is the sergeant suspicious?

If you need a hint, please turn to page 54. For the solution, turn to page 58.

3 WHICH TEAM DOES THAT GUY PLAY FOR?

MS. NASH: This is as far as I can take you by car. You go the rest of the way on foot. Libby, you bring your binoculars like I told you?

LIBBY: Uh huh. Got 'em right here.

MS. NASH: You too, Travis? Good. Now listen up, both of you. The Montrose ball field is on the other side of that hill. There's a game going on there right now, and I've had reports that one of the teams is cheating, but I don't know which one. Either the Montrose Pirates or the . . . what's the visiting team? Oh yeah, the Linwood Huskies. One of them is using a player that's too old to play Little League. A real big kid. Blond.

TRAVIS: This big kid, Ms. Nash. He plays shortstop, right?

MS. NASH: He plays every position. But the way you pick him out is that he's at least a head taller than everybody else. Now here's the drill. You climb the little fence there and go up to the hill. When you're at the top, crouch down. Stay in the long grass and use the binoculars. Don't let anybody see you! As soon as you figure out which team this tall, blond kid plays for, get back down here to the car. Now off you go!

LIBBY: (to Travis) Holy smoke! Almost forgot! (Yells back to car) Hey, Ms. Nash! Ms. Nash! What color are the team uniforms, so we know which is which?

MS. NASH: The Montrose Pirates are red and white. I don't know about the Linwood team. Now get going!

TRAVIS: This should be close enough. At least no one can see us. And look! There's the big kid. You can't miss him! He's coming up to bat right now. And see? See when he took off his battin' helmet. Blond hair! That's him all right. And. . . .

LIBBY: Travis. . . .

TRAVIS: Boy, that first pitch was right across the plate and he just stared at it. He's. . . .

LIBBY: Travis. . . .

TRAVIS: Another one! He's going to strike out! He. . . .

LIBBY: Travis!

TRAVIS: What?

LIBBY: Both teams have red and white uniforms.

TRAVIS: Omigosh! He just struck out! What did you say?

LIBBY: The big blond kid. What color is his uniform?

TRAVIS: Uh . . . uh . . . red and white. Just like Ms. Nash said so he must be playing for the Montrose Pirates.

LIBBY: Travis. The other team. What color is their uniform.?

TRAVIS: Red and white. But what's the . . . oh, oh.

LIBBY: Oh, oh indeed! Now we got to figure out . . .

What was that? I missed it?

TRAVIS: The kid battin' right after the big blond one. He's got a. . . . Yes! A home run! If that big kid had got on base, they'd have two runs right now!

LIBBY: Big deal, Travis. That doesn't tell us which team the big kid is playing for. There's red and white uniforms on both sides. And no names on them that we can see from here!

17

We can't even see the scoreboard from here!

TRAVIS: Relax and enjoy the game, Libby. All we have to do is wait for the other team to get a hit, and then we'll know which side the blond kid plays for.

How can Travis and Libby tell
which team the tall, blond kid plays for?

If you need a hint, please turn to page 54. For the solution, turn to page 59.

4 THE CASE OF THE VERY BUSY BOOKWORM

LINDSAY BURGESS: Good morning. Special Claims. Lindsay Burgess speaking.

ASHLEY A. ASHLEY: I want the Plague, Pestilence, and Pitfall Insurance Company. Who are you?

LINDSAY BURGESS: This is Plague, Pestilence, and Pitfall. You have reached the claims department.

ASHLEY A. ASHLEY: Well it's about time! That's what I've got. A claim. Now write this down!

LINDSAY BURGESS: Sir. . . .

ASHLEY A. ASHLEY: I'm a bibliophile. Can you spell that? B-I-B-L-I-O-P-H-I-L-E. It means a person who likes books. And you want to know why I've got a claim? I've got a book-worm in my library; that's why!

LINDSAY BURGESS: Sir. . . .

ASHLEY A. ASHLEY: I found him—this is what really makes me furious—I found him in my very valuable first edition of *The Guinness*

Book of Records! Curled up all nice and comfy on page one ninety-eight! The very last page of the book. He'd eaten his way right through. Are you writing this down like I told you?

LINDSAY BURGESS: Sir, please! You have to tell me your name before I can help you.

ASHLEY A. ASHLEY: My name is Ashley A. Ashley. The 'A' stands for Abcdarian, A-B-C-darian. That's a person who likes alphabetical order. I like alphabetical order. My mother and father were abcdarians too. Now get your checkbook out!

LINDSAY BURGESS: Uh . . . sir. My department is set up to handle very unusual situations. Are? . . .

ASHLEY A. ASHLEY: Isn't a bookworm unusual enough? Now listen to what I say. This . . . this . . . bookworm has eaten a tunnel right through my first edition of *The Guinness Book of Records*. The tunnel starts in a copy of the *Fowler Book of Records*, and then goes right through to the *Guinness* book beside it. You see, all my record books are lined up so they stand side by side. It's very neat. Are you sure you understand all this?

LINDSAY BURGESS: Mr. Ashley, I have your policy on my computer screen now. Yes, it shows you have a first edition of *The Guinness Book of Records*. It was published in August, 1955, and yes, it has one hundred ninety-eight pages. You have insured the book for ten dollars a page. Goodness! That is a valuable book!

ASHLEY A. ASHLEY: That is why I told you to get your checkbook out. Your calculator too. One hundred ninety-eight pages at ten dollars a page. Punch it in. That's what you owe me!

LINDSAY BURGESS: I'm afraid not, Mr. Ashley. From what you have told me, my calculator says we only owe you ten dollars.

ASHLEY A. ASHLEY: What!

How does Lindsay Burgess know
that Ashley A. Ashley is trying to cheat Plague,
Pestilence, and Pitfall Insurance Company?

If you need a hint, please turn to page 55. For the solution, turn to page 59.

5 WHO WAS GUARDING THE PRISONERS?

COLONEL BASSO: Close that door, soldier!

SOLDIER: Yes, sir, Colonel Basso, sir!

COLONEL BASSO: Now, soldier. Let's hear that report you have in your hand there.

SOLDIER: Yes, sir, Colonel Basso, sir!

On June 28, two prisoners were placed in a special cell at the east end of the prison compound. At some time between ten P.M. and midnight on a day in July—it is not known what day—both prisoners escaped. They dug a tunnel from the cell, out underneath the wall of the compound. One prisoner has been recaptured.

That is all I have, Colonel Basso, sir!

COLONEL BASSO: Very good, thank you soldier.

Captain Treble! It was one of your people on sentry duty the night of the escape. The reason we're here is to find out who it was. What have you got to tell us?

CAPTAIN TREBLE: Yes sir, Colonel, I realize it was one of my people on duty. It was either Private Allegro or Private Rondo. Unfortunately, both have disappeared. We haven't found them yet.

COLONEL BASSO: Quiet in here or I'll clear the room! Go on.

CAPTAIN TREBLE: Private Allegro was on sentry duty until midnight on odd days of the month; that is, the first, the third, the fifth and so on. Private Rondo was on duty on even days.

COLONEL BASSO: I see. I'm not impressed, Captain Treble. Bring the prisoner front and center.

Prisoner! I understand you started digging the tunnel on the very day you were put in the cell. Is that right?

PRISONER: Yeah. Four feet that first day. Four feet the next day. Four the day after that. In fact. . . .

COLONEL BASSO: Four feet, you say?

PRISONER: Yeah. Every day. Only trouble was, the tunnel kept fallin' in on us. We'd get in there and dig out the four feet. Next day, we'd get back to the head of the tunnel and find out that two feet had fallen back in. Happened ever' single day.

COLONEL BASSO: Captain, according to my information, the wall of the compound is exactly twelve feet from this cell.

CAPTAIN TREBLE: Yes, sir.

COLONEL BASSO: And the wall is exactly one foot thick.

CAPTAIN TREBLE: Yes, sir.

COLONEL BASSO: Then all you need is calendar, and maybe a pencil, to figure out who was on sentry duty when the prisoners got out.

Who was on sentry duty when the prisoners escaped:
Private Allegro or Private Rondo?

If you need a hint, please turn to page 55. For the solution, turn to page 60.

6 A DILEMMA ON THE FOURTEENTH GREEN

COMMENTATOR: That concludes the action here on the tenth. Just a reminder that you're watching UCTV, Channel 7 coverage of the Greater Mulligan Ladies Invitational Golf Tournament. Let's go now to the fourteenth green, where Tom Driver and Sheila Parr have an interesting situation for us. Are you there Tom and Sheila?

TOM DRIVER: Thanks, Morgan. We have a most interesting development here on the fourteenth. The paper bag you see there on your screen has a golf ball in it! Arethra Sandtrap made a magnificent tee shot just a few minutes ago. Right on the green. But the wind blew that paper bag onto the green and the ball rolled into it! Sheila?

SHEILA PARR: Right, Tom. The bag came from the crowd here at the fourteenth. From where I stand it looks like it had popcorn in it. Very light paper. The wind today could easily move an empty bag like that. Now the problem Arethra has is that. . . .

TOM DRIVER: Sorry to cut in, Sheila. It looks like the

judges are about to rule what Arethra can do. Can you hear what they're saying?

SHEILA PARR: Tom, the judges have ruled that Arethra can not touch the ball. That is, she can't take it out of the bag!

That's a tough ruling, Tom. Could cost her the lead!

TOM DRIVER: Is she upset, Sheila?

 SHEILA PARR: Actually, no, Tom. She's seems very calm about it and . . . goodness sake! She's kneeling down beside the bag! You can see that on your screen, can't you?

TOM DRIVER: Yes, I can. And she's . . . oh wow!

SHEILA PARR: Those of you watching at home have never seen a golfing mystery solved this way before, but Arethra Sandtrap has done it! The bag is gone, and she has not touched the ball!

How did Arethra Sandtrap solve the paper bag
problem without touching the ball?

If you need a hint, please turn to page 55. For the solution, turn to page 60.

7 THE CASE OF QUEEN VICTORIA'S JEWELRY BOX

BAILIFF: Next case. Docket Number seven, four, seven, four. The State vs. Mr. Fred D. Septive. The charge is grand larceny. Judge Julio Vasquez presiding. How do you plead, Mr. Septive?

FRED D. SEPTIVE: How do you think I would plead to such a silly charge? Larceny means cheating and here I am, an honest businessperson, trying to make an honest dollar selling rare items. I sell antiques. Rare antiques. I have. . . .

JUDGE VASQUEZ: Mr. Septive. Mr. Fred D. Septive. This is, what, the third time we've met in the past year? It seems to me the first time was when you were selling keyholes to little old ladies who worried about burglars.

And the second time it was your invention, your journey into chemistry, wasn't it? If I remember correctly, you claimed to have invented a liquid so powerful it could melt anything it touched. And you had the nerve to bring a bottle of it into court here.

And now what do we have? Jewelry boxes. No, I'm

wrong . . . one jewelry box. A jewelry box that you would have us believe was the personal property of Queen Victoria of England.

FRED D. SEPTIVE: A fine piece of work, Your Honor. Very rare. She was the only queen ever to be named Victoria.

JUDGE VASQUEZ: Mr. Septive, are you suggesting I don't know my history? Indeed she was the only English queen with that name. Became queen in 1837 when she was still a young girl . . . but this jewelry box you say is hers . . . I have to admit, it really is quite beautiful. Hmmmm. About the size of a microwave. That's big.

And here's her name on the lid. Victoria the First. Hmmmm. It looks like the word Victoria has been made out of pearls— if those are real pearls. And the word First . . . I'd say those are rubies. Real rubies? . . . I don't know, Mr. Septive.

FRED D. SEPTIVE: Your honor, this is definitely no ordinary jewelry box. Lift the lid! Open it up!

JUDGE VASQUEZ: All right.

Mr. Septive, do you really expect me to believe that there were music boxes back in 1837?

FRED D. SEPTIVE: Oh, Judge Vasquez, of course. Music boxes were around long before that. That's a well-known fact.

JUDGE VASQUEZ: Well . . . perhaps you're right. But there's still something about this case that bothers me. I just can't seem to put my finger on it.

What clue should help the judge to figure out whether or not the jewelry box really belonged to the queen?

If you need a hint, please turn to page 55. For the solution, turn to page 61.

8 THE MAN WHO CAME HOME TOO LATE

NARRATOR: Lavawna Jefferson moved her wheelchair to the desk and waited for the man sitting across from her to finish wiping his glasses. He was nervous, and she didn't want to push him. Instead, she stared out the window and watched

the sky turn darker and darker. The forecast was right, she thought to herself. The freezing weather was about to turn into a storm. Just what she needed. Snow!

Finally, the man looked up and Lavawna spoke.

LAVAWNA: Those look like very strong glasses, Mr. Tribelli. Do you wear them all the time?

MR. TRIBELLI: Er . . . from the morning—from the minute I get up in the morning.

LAVAWNA: Then of course you had them on when you saw the intruder run out the back door.

MR. TRIBELLI: Oh, oh yes.

LAVAWNA: But you only saw the back of him?

MR. TRIBELLI: That's right. Still, I got a good look. He had a bomber jacket on. Short, brown leather. And jeans with a rip in the seat. Dark hair. He's about the same height as me.

It's like I said before. He must have run from upstairs when he heard me come into the house. Or maybe he saw me walking up the street from the bus stop. If I had come home just a minute earlier, maybe even twenty seconds, my wife would still be . . . alive!

NARRATOR: Lavawna went back to staring out the window while Mr. Tribelli covered his face with his hands and sobbed.

Two thoughts were going through Lavawna's mind. One was that she wanted to get home before the storm broke because it was hard to move her wheelchair in snow. The other thought was about the big hole in Mr. Tribelli's story.

What is the big hole in Mr. Tribelli's story?

If you need a hint, please turn to page 56. For the solution, turn to page 61.

9 THERE'S A BODY AT HICKORY DICKORY DOCK

CHENG: Back this way, Lieutenant De Vere. We've got to go in the back door. From the alley.

DE VERE: What's the matter, Cheng? Won't the key work on the front door?

CHENG: It's locked with a dead bolt, sir. You know, one of those sliding things, you lock from the inside?

DE VERE: I know what a dead bolt is, Cheng.

CHENG: Yes, sir! I mean sorry, sir. I mean, yes sir!

DE VERE: It's okay, Cheng, stay cool. You've done a good job. Look, everybody's got to be a rookie at some point.

CHENG: Yes, lieutenant.

DE VERE: And you've done everything properly. You looked in the front window of Hickory Dickory Dock here, and saw old Mr. Pendulum on the floor.

CHENG: That's right, sir.

DE VERE: And here in the alley, that's where you caught the two suspects that are now at the station.

CHENG: That's right, sir. The male suspect said he's never come to this part of the city before because of all the crime, but he's got this clock he wants fixed. So he brings it to Hickory Dickory Dock here, and the front door's locked. He's not surprised because it's after closing time so he goes around to the back and sees the woman coming out the back door. Now she says she comes here to Mr. Pendulum all the time. Otherwise, her story's exactly the same. Only she says it was the guy coming out the door.

Both of them were carrying these expensive-looking clocks.

DE VERE: I see. Very well, open up. Let's go in. You found him here?

CHENG: Mr. Pendulum? Yes, sir.

DE VERE: Take a good look around, Officer Cheng. Just standing here should give you a pretty good idea which one of your two suspects was here in Mr. Pendulum's clock shop.

Which suspect is Lieutenant De Vere talking about?

If you need a hint, please turn to page 56. For the solution, turn to page 62.

10 HAS ANYBODY SEEN TIPPI BURNSIDE?

NARRATOR: Alfred Price-Jones walked up one aisle of the huge greenhouse, and then down the one next to it. He moved very slowly. Because of his allergies, Alfred Price-Jones wanted to be sure his feet didn't stir up the dust. He was also careful not to brush up against the plants drooping over the shelves and into the aisles.

Just being in the greenhouse was an act of courage for him. Pollen made his whole body swell up, and made it hard for him to breathe. Most of the time, ordinary dust did the same thing. Alfred Price-Jones knew he could stay in here for only a few minutes.

Still, he had to check the greenhouse himself, because Tippi Burnside had been seen here last night at seven o'clock. No one had seen her since. It was now two A.M. and, officially, Tippi Burnside was missing.

The last person to see her was sitting outside in Alfred Price-Jones's squad car. He was a worker here at the greenhouse. The night man, he called himself. According to him, Tippi had wandered into the greenhouse last night around seven P.M., while he was watering the plants. He'd told her to leave, he said. Nobody was allowed into the greenhouse without permission. Nobody. The man said he didn't know where she went after that.

Alfred Price-Jones paused in the doorway. His eyes were beginning to water now. Soon, he knew, his nose would plug up and he'd start to cough and sneeze. He held his breath and took one last look around. Even though he was in for some agony, the visit had been worth the trouble. There was no doubt now that the greenhouse worker had a lot of explaining to do.

Why is Alfred Price-Jones suspicious of the greenhouse worker's story?

If you need a hint, please turn to page 56. For the solution, turn to page 62.

11 THE CASE OF THE CULTIVATOR KILLING

NARRATOR: She was driving very slowly down Alban Street, looking for Number thirty-nine, but even so, Nicole Bernard's car seemed to make a lot of unnecessary noise. When she pulled up in front of Number Thirty-nine, Nicole was relieved to turn the key. She sat for a few seconds enjoying the quiet, sunny morning. She might have sat there even longer, but her attention was caught by someone at the house.

At the end of the little sidewalk leading into Number Thirty-nine, in the shade of the old house, Nicole could see the bottom of a pair of green shorts, and beneath them, the soles of a pair of green shoes. Someone, with her back to the street, was digging in the flower bed. Whoever it was, apparently didn't hear Nicole arrive, for the green shorts and green shoes stayed right in position.

NICOLE: Er . . . er . . . Mrs. Majeski?

MRS. MAJESKI: Oh! Oh! Holy COW! You scared me! I . . . I. . . . Look! If this is your

idea of a joke I'm not laughing! Do you cops always sneak up on innocent citizens like this? I mean. . . . Holy cow!

NICOLE: Mrs. Majeski! I'm sorry! I'm sorry. I didn't mean to sneak up! I'm . . . I'm Officer Bernard. From the coroner's office. It's . . . it's . . . I'm sorry, it's about your brother. You know the hearing starts next week.

MRS. MAJESKI: Yes, yes, yes. I know, I know. Whew! My heart's still pounding! You know, what you should do is have the hearing right here on the sidewalk, 'cause what you did to me just now is what he did. Sneaked up on me, the idiot—well, wait a minute! I don't actually know that he was sneaking up. All I know is that I was weeding this flower bed that morning. Just like today. Same spot, same time, everything. And all of a sudden there's this shadow over me. Scared me out of my wits! So I swung! With a hand cultivator just like this one. See these three sharp prongs. Caught poor old Sully right on the side of the head, and. . . . Well, why am I telling you all this? You know it already.

What do you want anyway?

NICOLE: To be honest, Mrs. Majeski, I was only going to remind you that the hearing starts at nine o'clock, but now. . . . Mrs. Majeski, I think I have to take you downtown with me.

Nicole Bernard has found a flaw in Mrs. Majeski's story of how she came to hit her brother with a hand cultivator.

If you need a hint, please turn to page 57. For the solution, turn to page 63.

THE POISON ON THE CHAIR

EDDY CAMOUFLAGE: Eddy Camouflage speakin'.

CRYPTO: Eddy, this is Crypto.

EDDY CAMOUFLAGE: Don't talk! Just a minute!
Okay. The line's safe now. What's up?

CRYPTO: The meeting tonight. The Jurassic Society?

EDDY CAMOUFLAGE: Yeah?

CRYPTO: It's a set up. An assassination. One of the chairs
has contact poison on it. Whoever sits on it is a goner. One
touch on bare skin and that's it.

EDDY CAMOUFLAGE: Holy moly! We're talkin' terrorists
here! Who are they after?

CRYPTO: Dr. T-Rex. They've been out to get him for
months. You gotta figure out where he's gonna sit and then
get rid of that chair. And wear gloves!

EDDY CAMOUFLAGE: Yeah, but how?

CRYPTO: The table they're gonna use. It's a rectangle, right?
One person sits at each end and two people on each side?

EDDY CAMOUFLAGE: As a matter of fact, that's right.
Yeah let's see . . . yeah, Professor Fossil sits beside Mrs.

Raptor. He's on her right. They face the window.

CRYPTO: And the way I've got it, she's gonna be directly across from Captain Bronta. 'Zat right?

EDDY CAMOUFLAGE: Yeah, right across. And T-Rex is sittin' across from that nutcase, Stego.

CRYPTO: You mean Stego's at this meeting? You sure know how to make trouble for yourself, Eddy!

EDDY CAMOUFLAGE: Hey, I don't pick 'em! As far as I'm concerned they can take their whole society and. . . .

CRYPTO: Eddy, c'mon. We only got a couple hours. Now, what d'ya know 'bout Walter Extinct?

EDDY CAMOUFLAGE: Not a lot. He's part of the meeting, we know that. And he'll be sitting closer to T-Rex than he will be to Stego. He doesn't like Stego, but who does?

CRYPTO: Then you got it!

EDDY CAMOUFLAGE: Got what?

CRYPTO: Ya' can figure out where Dr. T-Rex is gonna sit.

EDDY CAMOUFLAGE: I can?

Help Eddy Camouflage prevent the assassination of Dr. T-Rex.
Figure out where Dr. T-Rex is going to be sitting.

you need a hint, please turn to page 57. For the solution, turn to page 63.

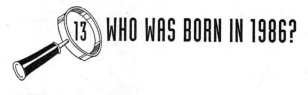

13 WHO WAS BORN IN 1986?

SPENSER: All right, we know why we're here. Today's date is April 1, 2002. It's the day that we are supposed to give a million dollar bond to whichever one of this kooky bunch was born in 1986. Let's collate our information and figure out which one it is. Since I've got the floor, I'll go first.

MILTON: I have a question.

BRONTE: Oh, no!

SPENSER: Don't tell me! You don't understand collate, right? It means "put together," like the pieces of a jigsaw puzzle.

MILTON: No, no. What do you mean, you've "got the floor?"

BRONTE: Oh Milton! Are you going to let him do this again, Spenser? He's always . . .

MILTON: You don't have the floor. We've all got the floor. Otherwise we'd fall through to the basement.

SPENSER: Milton! One more dumb-dumb and you will be in the basement! Now since you've got the floor—as usual—tell us what you have and we'll collate it with our information.

MILTON: Uh . . . uh . . . yeah. Collate. Whatever you say, Spenser. Okay. What I found out is that Andy has a twin brother.

BRONTE: That's it? That's all you found out?

MILTON: So! Did you do any better, smartypants?

SPENSER: Go ahead, Bronte.

BRONTE: First, I found out that Candy is a year younger

than Andy. And second, I found out Randy is a year younger than Candy.

SPENSER: Good work, Bronte.

MILTON: Hmmpf!

SPENSER: Let's see now. What I have is that Mandy is a year older than Lamont. Since we know that Randy celebrated his thirteenth birthday yesterday, I believe we have enough information.

MILTON: You mean, enough to collate?

BRONTE: Yes, Milton, enough to collate.

Which one of Randy, Candy, Mandy, Andy, and Lamont was born in 1986?

If you need a hint, please turn to page 57. For the solution, turn to page 64.

14 TAKING THE BANK ROBBER'S PICTURE

ANNOUNCER: Attention shoppers! All stores and services will be closing in five minutes. Central Market will be open again tomorrow from ten A.M. till ten P.M. Only three shopping days left before the big one!

CASSANDRA PORTENT: Detective Bastion! Oh, Detective Bastion!

DETECTIVE BASTION: Who are you?

CASSANDRA PORTENT: Oh, sorry! I'm Cassandra Portent. I'm with the security group here at Central Market.

DETECTIVE BASTION: I see. Is this about the bank robbery, or has something else happened?

CASSANDRA PORTENT: It's the robbery. I've got a woman in my office, says she took pictures of the robber leaving the bank!

DETECTIVE BASTION: Pictures of the guy? How could she? The robbery only happened two hours ago!

CASSANDRA PORTENT: Come on and talk to her yourself. She says she had just parked her car outside in the lot. Got lucky and found an empty spot right beside the Peel Street entrance. That's where the bank is—well, you know that—and she saw the guy coming out and took his picture.

DETECTIVE BASTION: How did she get the pictures developed so fast?

CASSANDRA PORTENT: In Central Market? Really, Detective. In this place you can get a film developed in half an hour. C'mon. She's up in my office.

Detective Bastion, this is Esther Ubiquity.

ESTHER UBIQUITY: Where have you been? I've got all this information for you and what happens? I sit here in this stuffy little office—you should clean this place a little better, young lady!—and nobody shows up! I even paid to develop these pictures myself!

DETECTIVE BASTION: Uh, Ms. Ubiquity. . . .

ESTHER UBIQUITY: It's Mrs! Mrs. My late husband, he didn't hold with all these fancy changes. That's what causing the country to fall apart, he said. You call me Mrs.!

DETECTIVE BASTION: Indeed. What I would like to know,

Mrs. Ubiquity, is what made you realize you should take these pictures right at that moment? I mean, do you carry your camera with you all the time?

ESTHER UBIQUITY: Young man, you listen to me. Being old doesn't mean I'm stupid, you know. I had the camera in my hand because I was taking it into that Skyway Photo place beside the bank to get it fixed. Flash doesn't work. See, there's this nice young man in that Skyway Photo— now there's a boy whose mother taught him some manners. That's why I always . . .

DETECTIVE BASTION: But Mrs. Ubiquity, how did you know who to photograph? According to other witnesses, some other people left the bank at the same time.

ESTHER UBIQUITY: But none of them took off a ski mask! What does somebody want with a ski mask in a bank! You think I don't know what I'm doing don't you! Well, wait till you see the pictures . . . after you pay me what it cost to get them developed!

DETECTIVE BASTION: Uh . . . Ms. Portent, may I speak to you outside for a minute?

CASSANDRA PORTENT: Are you thinking that she doesn't really have any pictures?

DETECTIVE BASTION: Oh, I'm sure she got the pictures, all right. But not of the bank robber. I bet she's in cahoots with the guy!

Why does Detective Bastion believe that Esther Ubiquity is working with the bank robber?

If you need a hint, please turn to page 57. For the solution, turn to page 64.

HINTS

1. THE CASE OF THE BLUE TATTOO

Hold a pen or pencil in your right hand and then stand in front of a mirror.

2. THE CASE OF MR. COMATOSA'S NIGHTMARE

When you see someone sleeping, are you able to tell what they are dreaming?

3. WHICH TEAM DOES THAT GUY PLAY FOR?

At a baseball game, if the home team has 100 fans, and the visiting team has 10 fans, which group is able to make the most noise.

4. THE CASE OF THE VERY BUSY BOOKWORM

Place two books side by side on a shelf, with the spines facing you. Then ask yourself: Where is the last page of the book on the right?

5. WHO WAS GUARDING THE PRISONERS?

Draw a diagram to help solve this mystery. Also, check how many days there are in the month of June.

6. A DILEMMA ON THE FOURTEENTH GREEN

What can a match do to a paper bag, that it cannot do to a golf ball?

7. THE CASE OF QUEEN VICTORIA'S JEWELRY BOX

Why are queens and kings of a country given numbers like the First and the Second?

8. THE MAN WHO CAME HOME TOO LATE

On very cold days, why do people take off their glasses when they come in from outside?

9. THERE'S A BODY AT HICKORY DICKORY DOCK

You are alone in a store. The front door is locked. Two people come to the door at different times. One is a complete stranger. The other is somebody you have met before. What would you do?

10. HAS ANYBODY SEEN TIPPI BURNSIDE?

What did the greenhouse worker say he was doing when he saw Tippi Burnside?

11. THE CASE OF THE CULTIVATOR KILLING

Think about sunlight, and think about where Mrs. Majeski was working when Nicole drove up.

12. THE POISON ON THE CHAIR

A diagram of a rectangular table will help a lot.

13. WHO WAS BORN IN 1986?

Start by figuring out the year in which Randy was born.

14. TAKING THE BANK ROBBER'S PICTURE

Is there more daylight in June or in December?

SOLUTIONS

1. THE CASE OF THE BLUE TATTOO

Mr. Gray said he saw the shoplifter put the hairdryer into the front of his shirt. Therefore the shoplifter was facing the  mirror. When you face a mirror, the reflection makes your left arm look like your right one. If the shoplifter's tattoo appeared on the right, it was actually on his left arm. It appears Mr. Gray forgot about that when he picked a suspect.

2. THE CASE OF MR. COMATOSA'S NIGHTMARE

If Mr. Comatosa had a nightmare and died from a heart attack during the nightmare, Mrs. Comatosa would not know what he was dreaming about.

3. WHICH TEAM DOES THAT GUY PLAY FOR?

In a game between teams from different towns, the hometown fans usually make the most noise because there are more of them. After the tall, blond player struck out, the next batter—from the same team—hit a home run, and the crowd noise was very loud. Travis wants to wait until a player from the other team makes a big hit. If the crowd noise is quieter, then it's very likely the blond player is one of the Montrose Pirates because this is the Montrose home field. If the noise is louder, then the big player is one of the Linwood Huskies.

4. THE CASE OF THE VERY BUSY BOOKWORM

Ashley A. Ashley says the *Guinness* book and the *Fowler* book stand side by side. Because he is an abcdarian, and keeps everything in alphabetical order, the *Fowler* book will be on the left of the

Guinness one. Therefore, if the bookworm started in the *Fowler* book and tunneled through to the *Guinness* book, page 198 will be the first page it comes to, not the last one. Since that's where Mr. Ashley found the worm, it means that only one page of the *Guinness* book has been damaged.

5. WHO WAS GUARDING THE PRISONERS?

It was Private Allegro. The prisoners had to dig a distance of thirteen feet to get underneath the wall. They dug four feet a day but two feet always caved in by the next day. That means their progress was two feet a day for five days, or ten feet. On the sixth day, they dug the usual distance, but this was enough to get outside before the tunnel caved in again, as it always did. If the prisoners started on the twenty-eighth of June, they were out before midnight on the third of July, an odd day of the month.

6. A DILEMMA ON THE FOURTEENTH GREEN

Arethra burned the bag!

7. THE CASE OF QUEEN VICTORIA'S JEWELRY BOX

Queens and kings are not called the First until there is another one with the same name. Both the judge and Fred D. Septive said that Victoria was the only English queen ever to have that name, so her jewelry box would only say "Victoria" on it, not "Victoria the First."

Music boxes, incidentally, were invented about fifty years before Queen Victoria was born. As for selling keyholes and powerful liquids, we're sure you caught on to those right away.

8. THE MAN WHO CAME HOME TOO LATE

If the weather was very cold, Mr. Tribelli's glasses would have been fogged up for the first minute or so after coming into the warm house. He would not have been able to see an intruder with the detail he describes.

9. THERE'S A BODY AT HICKORY DICKORY DOCK

Both suspects say they came to Hickory Dickory Dock after closing time. In a high crime area of town, Mr. Pendulum is not likely to open his door after hours for a stranger. But the woman suspect  says she comes to this clock store all the time. Lieutenant De Vere believes that Mr. Pendulum let her in and then bolted the door again. He suspects her of murdering Mr. Pendulum and then leaving by the back door.

10. HAS ANYBODY SEEN TIPPI BURNSIDE?

The greenhouse worker said he was watering the plants when he saw Tippi Burnside at seven P.M. That was only hours ago. Yet Alfred Price-Jones had to be careful not to brush against drooping plants or stir up dust. It seems the watering part of the worker's story is false.

11. THE CASE OF THE CULTIVATOR KILLING

Mrs. Majeski says that on a morning just like this one, and at the same time of day, she turned and swung at her brother with the hand cultivator when she was frightened by his shadow looming over her. However, Mrs. Majeski was working in the shade. She would not have seen a shadow.

12. THE POISON ON THE CHAIR

Professor Fossil sits on Mrs. Raptor's right on one side of the table, facing the window. Captain Bronta sits across from Mrs. Raptor. Since T-Rex sits across from Stego, they must be at the two ends of the table. Walter Extinct is going to sit closer to T-Rex than to Stego, so Extinct is then across from Professor Fossil, with T-Rex at the end between them. That's the chair Eddy has to get rid of.

13. WHO WAS BORN IN 1986?

Today's date is April 1, 2002, and yesterday Randy celebrated his thirteenth birthday. Randy, therefore, was born in 1989. He's a year younger than Candy so she was born in 1988. Candy is a year younger than Andy so he, and his twin, Lamont, were born in 1987. Since Mandy is a year older than Lamont, she was born in 1986 and gets the million dollar bond.

14. TAKING THE BANK ROBBER'S PICTURE

The bank robbery took place at about eight P.M., two hours before closing. Three days before Christmas the days are short and it would be dark in the  parking lot by eight P.M. A flash would be needed on a camera. Esther Ubiquity says her flash needs to be fixed so the pictures she has are probably of someone else, taken at another time. Detective Bastion believes she is trying to throw him off the trail of the real bank robber.